Best of
MORAL STORIES

TINY TOT

st of
STORIES

TINY TOT

Best of
MORAL STORIES

TINY TOT

Best of
MORAL
STORIES

TINY TOT PUBLICATIONS
INDIA

Best of
Moral Stories

© 2002 TINY TOT PUBLICATIONS
This Edition:- 2003

Retold & Edited by: Shyam Dua

Published By:

TINY TOT PUBLICATIONS

235, Jagriti Enclave,
Vikas marg,
Delhi-110092 (INDIA)
Ph.: 2216 7314, 2216 3582
Fax:- 91-11-22143023
email: tinytotpub@hotmail.com

ISBN : 81-7573-576-7

CONTENTS

S.no.		Page no.
1.	The Deaf Son-in-law	7
2.	The Boastful Wrestler	9
3.	Tenali Raman's NewAppointment	13
4.	Raju's Clever Plan	17
5.	Sonu and Monu	19
6.	The Loyal Servant	21
7.	The Thankful Ant	22
8.	The Proud Crow	23
9.	The Torn Painting	25
10.	Treasure in the Field	27
11.	The Donkey's Shadow	29
12.	The Lamb and the Wolf	31
13.	The Donkey's Burden	33
14.	Timid Minku	35
15.	The Cat's Bell	37
16.	The Scared Fox	40
17.	The Stag's Antlers	42

18. The Thankless Wolf............ 44

19. The Potter's Donkey........... 45

20. The Imitating Crow............ 47

21. The Shepherd Boy's Lesson.. 48

22. The Woodcutter's Axe........ 50

23. The Capseller's Trick.......... 52

24. The Proud Donkey............. 54

25. The Unfaithful Friend........ 56

26. The Clever Stork................ 58

27. The Monkey Judge............. 59

28. The Kind Lion................... 60

29. The Two Goats.................. 61

30. The Golden Eggs................ 62

31. The Dog in the Stream........ 63

32. The Lazy Grasshopper........ 64

33. Dinner in the Town............ 66

34. The Race........................ 67

35. The Sour Grapes................ 69

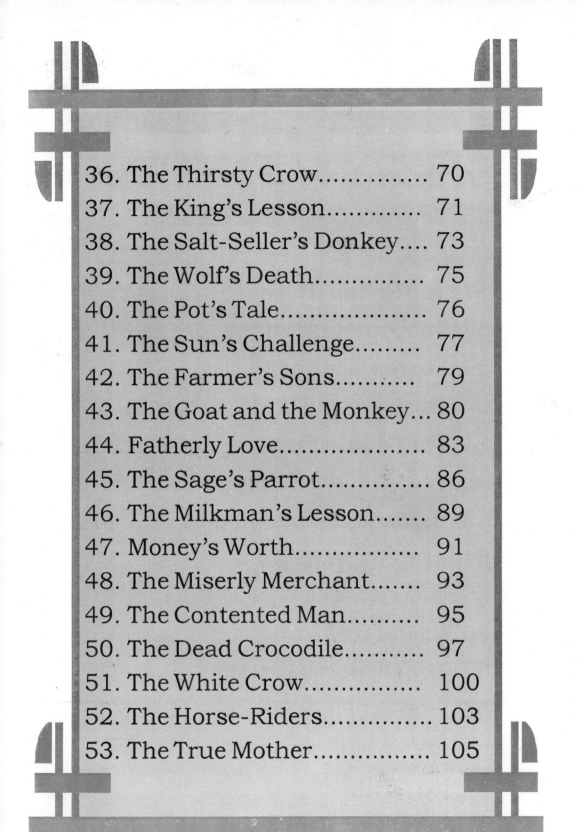

36. The Thirsty Crow............... 70

37. The King's Lesson............. 71

38. The Salt-Seller's Donkey.... 73

39. The Wolf's Death............... 75

40. The Pot's Tale................... 76

41. The Sun's Challenge......... 77

42. The Farmer's Sons........... 79

43. The Goat and the Monkey... 80

44. Fatherly Love................... 83

45. The Sage's Parrot.............. 86

46. The Milkman's Lesson....... 89

47. Money's Worth................. 91

48. The Miserly Merchant....... 93

49. The Contented Man......... 95

50. The Dead Crocodile.......... 97

51. The White Crow............... 100

52. The Horse-Riders.............. 103

53. The True Mother................ 105

54. The Son's Lesson................ 107

55. The Astrologer's Prediction.. 110

56. A Riddle to Solve................ 112

57. The Helpful Dove............... 115

58. The Proud Elephant........... 117

59. For the Good of All............. 120

60. The Hare and the Ass......... 122

61. The Jamun Tree................ 125

62. The Friendly Elephant........ 126

63. Befriending the Jackal........ 128

64. Lazy Stomach................... 131

65. Miser's Money.................. 133

66. Raghu Goes to Jail............. 135

67. The Donkey's Disguise........ 138

68. The Wet Monkey................ 140

69. Praise be on the Lord.......... 142

The Deaf Son-in-law

Tota Ram got married to a beautiful girl. No one knew how, but after marriage, he lost his hearing. Initially he would hear a little less. Gradually it grew worse and soon he grew totally deaf. Now even if someone screamed into his ears, he could not hear any thing. This problem led Tota Ram to isolate himself. He stopped going out and meeting people. He could not hear, so conversation was not possible for him at all.

One morning a messenger came to Tota Ram. He told him that his father-in-law was seriously ill. No one knew if he would survive. Tota Ram did not know what to do. If he did not visit his ailing father-in-law then everyone would think he was too proud or that he felt nothing for his elders. Tota Ram thought hard. Then he wrote down a list of questions and answers, he expected in a conversation there. He wrote:

I'll ask, "Father, how are you feeling now ?"

He'll say, "I am better now, son."

I'll say, "I am so glad about it. Which medicine are you taking?"

He will name the medicine.

I'll say, "That's the best for you."

Then I'll ask, "Which doctor is treating you?"

He'll name the doctor.

Then I'll say, "That's great. Leave everything in his hands. He'll soon rid you of all your problems."

So Tota Ram learnt all the points of the conversation he wished to have with his father-in-law. Then Tota

Ram left for his father-in-law's village. On reaching his father-in-law's house, he touched his feet and asked, "Father, how are you feeling now?"

Tota Ram's father-in-law groaned and said, "I won't live for long, son."

As Tota Ram couldn't hear, he thought he had received the expected answer. Then he commented, "I am so glad about it. Which medicine are you taking ?"

Hearing Tota Ram's comment, his father-in-law got irritated, so he said, "Poison."

Deaf Tota Ram assumed he had got the expected reply again, so he said, "That's the best for you."

His father-in-law stared at Tota Ram in shock. He did not know of Tota Ram's deafness, so he could

not understand his comments. Then Tota Ram enquired, "Which doctor is treating you ?"

In an angry voice, the old man said, "Yamraj, the God of Death."

To this, deaf Tota Ram said, "That's great. Leave everything in his hands. He'll soon rid you of all your problems."

This time Tota Ram's father-in-law could not control his anger. He got out of the bed and pulled Tota Ram with the collar and sent him out of his house. Poor deaf Tota Ram did not realize what he had done to deserve such treatment.

| MORAL : Do not be sure of all your future plans. |

The Boastful Wrestler

Once a tall, handsome, well-built wrestler visited a king's royal court. He said to the king, "Your Majesty, I am very healthy and my body is full of strength. I can drink hundred litres of milk a day. I can fight ten wrestlers at one go single handedly. I had once lifted a mountain on my head and my fights with lions are well-known."

The king heard all the wrestler's tales and seeing him, he was impressed. He gave the wrestler a post to work on. The king was sure that some day his services would be needed. The wrestler did not do much. Mostly he used to tell his boastful tales and used to eat a lot, sleep a lot and impress the king with false tales.

There was a high hill near the kingdom's border. It so happened that wild animals from the forests on the hill slopes started entering the villages at night. They used to spoil the standing crops and often

attack poultry and cattle for food. The people were scared to go out at night due to fear of their attacks. This news reached the king's ears. He remembered that the wrestler had told him many of his tales of valour. He called the wrestler and said, "You had once claimed that you had lifted a mountain on your head. Now is the time to prove yourself. There is a forested hill near our kingdom's border. You must lift it and shift or throw it somewhere far from us. This way my people will no longer be troubled by the animals from these forests."

"Yes, Your Majesty. We'll go there immediately but before that I want to eat something." So he had a heavy lunch and then accompanied the king and the courtiers to where the hill stood. Once there he took off his shirt, flexed his muscles and exercised a bit. Then he said to the king, "I am ready to lift the hill. Your Majesty, tell me, should I throw it into the next kingdom or to the country across the sea ? I can do as you wish but first you'll have to call your men. So that they dig the hill out of the firm ground before I lift it on my head."

"But you said that you could lift a mountain !" exclaimed the king.

"That's right, Your Majesty. I can lift this hill on my head but I can't dig it out of the ground. I never claimed I could do that."

Hearing this, the king felt dejected. He had been cheated by a man who told false tale. The wrestler was of no use at all.

MORAL : False claims get you nowhere.

Tenali Raman's New Appointment

Tenali Raman was a clever minister and also a court jester in the kingdom of Vijaynagar. Once he was given the appointment of being a judge. Here is how it all happened.

An old, poor woman lived in Vijaynagar. Once four thieves came to her house and said, "We are pilgrims and we are tired after travelling so long. We want to rent a room in your house."

The old woman agreed and the thieves started living with her. One night they gave her a pot whose mouth was shut with a cloth and string.

"What is this ?" she enquired.

"A pot full of gold coins," one of the thieves replied.

"A pot full of gold coins! Who are you ? Are you thieves ?" she exclaimed.

"No, we are pilgrims as you know. You have seen us going out every night. We go to various temples at night to sing *bhajans* in *jagrans*. People give us money for that. This is our saving. Keep it with you. Please promise us that you will give the pot to us only if all four of us ask for it together."

The old woman believed them. She hid the pot in a hole in the ground behind her hut.

After some days when one night the thieves were returning home, they saw a woman selling butter-milk. They wanted to buy some, so as they were near the old woman's house, they sent one of them to get the money from the pot. The thief, who went to get the money, met the old woman. "Please give the pot to me. We need money to buy the butter-milk."

It was dark outside, so the old woman asked from  the door, "Can I give the pot to him ?"

"Yes, please give it to him," they yelled back.

The old woman dug out the pot of gold coins and gave it to the greedy thief. He took the pot and slipped away in the cover of darkness. The three thieves

kept waiting but he did not
return. At last, the three
of them went to the old
woman and asked,
"Where is the pot of
gold coins?"

"I gave it to the other
one who came in."

"But we made you
promise you'll give
the pot only when all
four of us are
together," they said.

"But you yelled back that I could give it to him !"

"No, No,.. That's cheating. We want our money back."

The argument grew tense. Soon the sun rose and
the neighbours heard their raised voices. A crowd
gathered. Tenali Raman was passing by. Hearing
the argument he, too, went to see. The king was
taking a morning stroll and he, too, reached the
place.

When the king arrived, Tenali Raman told him what
had happened and said, "Your Majesty, the old
woman cannot be blamed. She cannot be guilty."

"Well, then prove it to me," the king ordered. Tenali
Raman made the three men step aside. He listened
to their story once more. After hearing the whole

event, Tenali Raman shouted at them, "Didn't you make the old woman promise to give you the money only when all four of you were present ?"

"Y…yes, S…sir," the men stammered in fear.

"And you are asking for it now. How many are you ?"

"Three, S…sir," they replied.

"You are three men not four. Where's the fourth man ? How can you claim your money from the old

woman when the fourth man is missing ?"

This logical questioning did not let the thieves reply. Soon they confessed they were thieves. They were sent to prison and the old woman thanked Tenali Raman.

The king was impressed and appointed Tenali Raman as the judge of his kingdom.

MORAL : Cheaters are always losers.

Raju's Clever Plan

Raju was a ten year old village boy. One morning his father called him and gave him a silver box. He said, "Raju, now you are old enough to help me in my work. I want you to take this silver box to Uncle Mani who lives in the next village. It is about five kilometres away. I want you to leave now, so that you can be back before sundown. I want you to be alert and careful on the way."

"Yes, father, I'll take this silver box as you say. I'll be back soon," Raju said.

So Raju left for the next village. He reached Uncle Mani's house. Uncle Mani took the silver box from Raju. Raju rested for an hour and ate delicious lunch prepared by Aunt Parvati. Then Uncle Mani said, "Raju, I have taken what was inside the box.

Go back with this silver box now. Be careful not to lose this costly box on the way."

So Raju took leave with the silver box in his hand. As Raju walked through a woodland, he felt someone was following him. Soon Raju heard foot steps. Suddenly he saw a man at a distance following him behind the trees. Raju was sure he was a robber who wanted to take the silver box from him. So Raju started running. The robber also ran after him. Raju ran on and left the robber further away. On the way he saw a well. He drank some water

and sat down to rest. Just then Raju saw the robber coming down the path. Raju made a clever plan to save the silver box.

As soon as the robber came near Raju, he started crying loudly.

"What is wrong,

boy ?" the robber asked.

"I stopped to drink water from the well. My gold chain, gold watch and gold ring fell into the well. Oh! My father will beat me. I can't go home without them. Who will get them out for me ?" Raju cried.

The robber thought, "Surely these gold articles are expensive than the silver box in his hands. I must get them." The robber said, "Don't cry. I'll get these things for you." So the robber jumped into the well. Seeing the chance, Raju ran away home with the silver box in hand.

MORAL : Never let fear rule your brain.

Sonu and Monu

Once there lived two friends Sonu and Monu. They were very poor. They used to beg for alms. Sonu was blind while Monu was lame. He could not walk without help. One day Sonu heard that a large religious fair was being held in the next village. He said to Monu, "Friend, we must go to that fair. Many rich and saintly people will come there. We'll get a lot of alms."

"But Sonu, how can we go so far away ? You are blind so you can't see the way. I am lame so I can't walk for such a long distance."

Sonu smiled and said, "Don't be disheartened, Monu, I have found a way out. I am blind but I can walk to cover great distances. You cannot walk as you are lame, but you can show me the way to the fair. Now you can sit on my shoulders. You will see the way and tell me which way to go while I'll be your legs to carry you to the fair."

So the two friends went to the fair together and enjoyed themselves.

MORAL : Help others to help yourself.

The Loyal Servant

Once a king became friendly with a monkey. He used to be with the king all the time.

One afternoon the king was taking a nap in his chamber. Just then a fly came in through the open window. It buzzed around the king's bed and finally settled on the king's nose. The loyal monkey was sitting at the king's bedside as a bodyguard. When he saw the fly, he waved it away with his hand. The fly flew off and came back to sit on the

king's nose once again. Now the monkey used his handkerchief to wave it away. The third time the fly came back on the king's nose, the monkey grew very angry. He pulled out his sword and struck at the disturbing fly. The swift fly flew off again.

Alas ! the sword did not strike the fly. It struck and cut off the sleeping king's nose. The king woke up yelling in pain.

MORAL: Everyone cannot do every task.

The Thankful Ant

Once an ant fell into a pond. She was drowning. A dove saw the drowning ant. He broke a leaf from the tree branch and threw it near the ant in the water. The ant struggled and got onto the leaf. As the leaf floated to the pond side, the ant also reached there safely and climbed off the leaf. She had been saved by the dove's kind act.

Many days went past. One afternoon the ant was crawling on the forest floor looking for food. She saw the dove sitting on a nearby bush. She was about to call him when she spotted a man. He had a gun in his hand and he was aiming it at the dove. The ant realized that the dove's life was in danger so the ant quickly climbed to his foot and bit hard. The man was in severe pain so he missed his aim as the gun went off in his hand. The sound of the gun made the dove sense the danger so he flew off. Thus, by helping the dove, the ant had expressed his thankfulness.

MORAL : One good deed deserves another.

The Proud Crow

Once a crow was flying over a village in search of food. Suddenly he spotted a piece of meat lying on the ground. He swooped down and picked it up in his beak. Then he flew to a high branch of a tree and sat there.

A hungry fox was passing by. She saw the juicy meat in the crow's beak and stopped. Her mouth watered at the sight. Soon the fox thought up a plan to get the meat. She went and sat down under the tree. She looked at the crow and said, "Hello, Mr. Crow! You are looking fine today." The crow did not speak.

"Where have you been so many days ? You are looking so much smarter than before. There's a certain style about your appearance."

The crow's heart filled with pride at such praises.

But he felt if he talked to the fox, the meat will fall to the ground. So the crow kept silent.

"Alas ! Spring is gone. In this hot summer, only your sweet song can make me happy. Will you sing a sweet love song to please me ?"

This time the proud crow could not contain himself. He opened his mouth wide to render a song and plop! The meat fell to the ground. The hungry fox leapt at the meat and ran off without looking back even once.

MORAL : Beware of the flatterers.

The Torn Painting

Once there was a king who loved to spend his free time in painting. Once he went on a hunting trip. After hunting for sometime he got tired. So he took his canvas, colours and paint brushes and went up a small hill. From there he saw a beautiful sight of sunset. He started painting it. Soon he had completed the painting. He started admiring his work from side to side. He moved a step to the right to look at it and then to the left. He stepped back to view his work. He kept stepping back without realizing that he was nearing the edge of a cliff.

On the hill slope a little shepherd boy was returning home with his flock of sheep. He saw that the king was stepping back and may fall off the cliff anytime. He rushed up the hill and tore off the beautiful painting. Seeing this the king ran to the painting to save it. He smacked the boy on his cheek.

"How dare you tear my beautiful painting?" the king cried in anger.

"Sir, I did it to save your life. Turn around and see. If you had taken even a single step back then you would have fallen to your death."

At this the king looked back and was shocked. Then he thanked the young shepherd. He took him to the palace where he was taught by teachers. As he grew up as a young man he was appointed the chief minister.

MORAL : Presence of mind helps when great plans fail.

Treasure in the Field

A farmer had three lazy sons. They never worked and always asked for money to spend. The farmer thought of teaching them a lesson.

One day he called his sons and said, "Sons, I am growing old now. I want to tell you a secret."

The boys grew curious and excited. When the farmer had got their attention, he said, "I have a treasure hidden in my field. I have forgotten where it is. You must dig up the field to find it."

The lazy but greedy sons got ready to do the work. Next morning they got up early. By evening, they had dug up the whole field but they found no treasure. In the evening, they went home and said. "Father, we are very tired. We dug up the whole field but found no treasure."

The old farmer smiled and said, "It does not matter, sons. Now the field is dug up. Why don't you sow some corns in it ?"

The sons agreed and soon they bought some corn seeds to sow in their field. A few weeks later, there were good rains. Soon the field was filled with golden corn cobs swaying in the breeze. Then the farmer said, "Sons, you must cut this lush crop and sell it in the market. Bring the money to me."

The sons went to the field and cut the standing corns. They sold it in the market and earned a thousand rupees. They took the money to their father.

The old farmer saw the money and said, "Sons, this is the treasure I told you about. This treasure was in the soil of the field. Your hard work dug it out. If you work like this every year, you'll get this treasure all your life."

The lazy sons understood what their father meant. From that day, they worked hard and earned their own money.

MORAL : Fruits of labour are sweet.

The Donkey's Shadow

Once a man wanted to go to a town far away from where he lived. As it was a hot summer day, he decided to hire a donkey to ride on.

The donkey and its master accompanied the man. The man rode on the donkey's back as its master led him on. As they walked on, it was soon noon time. They decided to stop and rest for lunch. There were no trees or shady place anywhere in sight. The man got off the donkey's back and sat in the shade made by the donkey's body. The master of the donkey also wanted to rest. He poked the man to stand up and said, "You cannot sit there. Let me sit in the donkey's shadow. After all I own the donkey so its shadow, too, is mine."

"How is that so ?" the man exclaimed. "I have paid you to hire this animal for the day, so today both the donkey and the donkey's shadow are for me to use."

"Don't try to be smart, you cannot ..."

And so the argument continued and heated up. The men kept arguing.

The donkey standing in the sun could not bear the heat for long, so he ran away in search of a shady spot. The fighting men did not realize that the donkey and the shadow they were fighting for, had left them.

MORAL : Fighting for trivia leads to loss of the true thing.

The Lamb and the Wolf

Once a young lamb felt very thirsty. He went to a stream to drink water. A thirsty and hungry evil wolf arrived at the same stream to quench his thirst. When he saw the lamb, he thought, "Oh, such a young lamb ! I'll trap him in my talks and then have him for lunch."

So the wolf went nearest to where the lamb was drinking water. He drank from the same side where the lamb was drinking. Then in an angry tone the wolf growled, "You there !"

The lamb looked up. The wolf said, "Why are you dirtying the water I am drinking ?"

"Oh, it can't be true. You see the water is flowing

down from your side towards me. Then how could I make dirty your water ?"

"Oh ! You dare to argue with me. You are as rude as when I met you a month ago."

"But how can that be ? I am just three weeks old. I was not even born then."

"Then it must have been your rude mother. I'll eat you up to punish her."

With these words, the wolf leapt on the young lamb and ate him up.

MORAL : Stay away from evil.

The Donkey's Burden

A merchant owned a donkey and a horse. Every-day he would load his goods on the backs of both the animals and take them to the market to sell.

One hot morning, the merchant had only a small amount of goods to carry. He made one large bundle of the goods and loaded it on to the donkey's back. Then he took his horse along and all the three left for the market. As they walked on, the donkey felt tired carrying the heavy load. So he went near the horse and said, "Friend, I am getting tired. Will you carry half the load for me ?"

"No way," the horse said. "It's your load so you must carry it on your

own. I won't share it."

The donkey did not comment back. It was nearing noon. The donkey could not bear the heat and the heavy load so he fell to the ground and fainted. Soon he was foaming at the mouth. The merchant took the donkey's load and put all of it on the horse back. The horse now had to carry the heavy goods. Then the horse realized how the poor donkey had suffered and the horse had to carry the goods all the way to the market on his own.

MORAL : **Sharing other's burden now will benefit us in the future.**

Timid Minku

Minku was a timid rabbit who lived in a forest. He was always nervous. Even the slightest noise or movement would make him panic-struck!

On a hot afternoon Minku was taking a nap under a shady mango tree. A ripe mango fell and hit Minku on the head. Minku jumped up in panic. He did not even wait to see what had hit him. He ran shouting, "Run ! Run ! The sky is falling."

His shouts alerted the squirrels and the birds. They followed Minku. On the way they met deers and bears and, as Minku told them, they also followed him with their families.

Seeing such a large group of animals, the elephant asked, "Why are all of you running away ?"

"You, too, run like us and try to save your life," replied a deer.

"But why?" enquired

the elephant.

"Minku told us that the sky is falling."

"Then we must go and tell the king."

So the herd of elephants went with the others. On the way the leopards, the foxes and the monkeys also joined them. The thundering of so many running feet was heard all over the forest. The zebras enquired, "Why are you fleeing so fast ?"

Out of them, a monkey replied, "We are going to the king. We must ask him to take us to a safe place. You see the sky is falling."

As the zebras joined the group, the wolves and the giraffes also went along.

Soon enough the large group of animals led by Minku reached the lion's den. The lion came out as he heard the noise of all animals. He roared in anger, "Why are all of you here ? Don't you have anything to do ?"

The zebra said, "Sir, we are here to tell you that we must leave the forest immediately."

"Why ?" the lion asked.

"The sky is falling sir," the wolf replied.

"And who told you so ?" the lion enquired.

"Minku, the rabbit," all the animals replied in unison.

"Minku, take me where you felt the sky falling," the lion said. Minku led the lion and the other animals to the mango tree. On enquiry, Minku told what had happened. When the lion saw the mango on the ground, he said, "This ripe mango fell on timid Minku's head and he thought that the sky was falling. He did not check what hit him. And all of you believe him without confirming the fact. Shame on all of you for disturbing the peace of the forest."

Minku and all the animals felt very embarrassed at their antics.

MORAL : Don't follow herd instinct.

The Cat's Bell

Long long ago, there lived a baker in a market. He sold sweets, cakes and some dairy products such as cheese and butter. But lately a large group of mice made his shop their house. Every night, when the shop closed, they would devour the cakes, butter and cheese kept in the shop. The baker was very worried. His friend suggested him to domesticate a cat to keep the mice away.

The baker got a cat and left it in the shop to catch the mice. Slowly the cat ate many of the mice. The mice were afraid to come out of their holes. Then they called a meeting. At the meeting, the elder one of them said, "Dear friends, we all are gathered here to find out a way to get rid of the cat."

"Yes," another one said. "If she keeps catching us we'll stop going out of the hole. We'll not get any food and, thus, we'll all die of starvation."

A young clever mouse stood up and said, "The cat prowls softly and takes us by surprise. We must tie a bell round her neck."

"Yes," another mouse said excitedly. "This way whenever she is near we'll hear the sound of bell round her neck and be warned."

All the mice grew cheerful. They all agreed with this idea and congratulated the clever mouse for the idea. Suddenly the elder mouse said, "The idea is

brilliant, I agree. But which of you will go to bell the cat ?"

At this question the noise died down. There was pin drop silence. No one had an answer as no one had thought about it. Meanwhile the elder mouse saw the cat coming slowly towards the mice. He jumped down the stage and ran away informing the others about the danger. So all the mice ran away to safe places.

MORAL : Be practical in your plannings.

The Scared Fox

Once a hungry fox saw a cock on a branch of a tree. As the fox was hungry, he thought of impressing the cock with some tale to trap it.

He approached the tree and said, "Dear cock, have you heard the latest?"

"What is it?" the cock enquired.

"A voice from the Heavens up above was heard yesterday. It announced that all animals and birds must now live in peace. They will now be friends and no one will harm the other. So come down to me. Let's be friends and shake hands in friendship."

The cock understood the fox's cunning plan. So the cock pretended to look far away and said, "Oh, yes! I have heard the news, too. I can see some of your other friends coming. Let them reach here then we will celebrate together."

"Friends ! Who are they ?" the fox asked.

"Oh! They are the hounds," replied the cock

At the hound's name, the fox got scared and started shivering in fear.

"Why do you look too scared ? They are our friends now," the cock said.

"But may be they have not heard the news yet." With these words, the scared fox fled the spot and the cock could not stop laughing.

MORAL : Don't believe words of the cunning.

The Stag's Antlers

Once a stag felt thirsty. He went to a lake to drink water. As he bent his neck to drink water, he looked at his reflection in water. On seeing his long, handsome antler, the stag thought. "What beautiful antlers. I have ! These shining, long antlers make me the most handsome of all in my herd."

And then he looked at his feet. "Oh ! Such ugly legs I have ! These legs are always dark and dirty. But anyway I have my beautiful antlers to feel happy about."

As the stag stood admiring his antler's reflection, he did not notice that some hunters had spotted him. The bark of the hounds alerted the stag.

The stag looked at the hunters. Then he ran off as fast as he could. He ran as fast as his legs could carry him. Soon he gained speed and left the hunters far behind. At a distance, the stag spotted some bushes and trees. He ran to the spot and hid behind the bushes. Soon the hunters and the

hounds came near the spot. The hounds sniffed and knew that the stag was hiding there. As the stag wanted to run off again, his antlers caught in the low branches of a tree. The stag could not run. Soon the hunters shot down the stag. The legs, the stag hated had saved him but his beautiful antlers had made the stag lose his life.

MORAL : Utility is important than beauty.

The Thankless Wolf

Once a wolf had a bone stuck in his throat. He could neither swallow it nor spit it out. He knew if he did not get it out, then he would not be able to eat either. Soon he would die of starvation.

The wolf went to a crane and said, "Please help me. A bone has stuck in my throat. Your long, spiny neck can get to reach it in my throat. Please pull the bone out of my throat. I'll reward you well."

The kind crane agreed to get the bone out. As the wolf sat with his wide open mouth, the crane put his beak into it and pulled out the bone.

Then the crane said, "I have got the bone out. Where is my reward you promised ?"

"Reward ! What reward !" the wicked wolf said. "I do not remember making any such promise." With these false words the thankless wolf left the crane's house.

MORAL : Wicked people are never thankful.

The Potter's Donkey

A poor potter owned a dog and a donkey. The dog used to guard the potter's house and the pots that were kept to dry in the courtyard. The potter used the donkey to carry the pots from the pottery to the market to sell them.

Once the donkey thought to himself, "I work so hard carrying the heavy loads to and fro to the market. I work in the heat and the cold, the whole day long but the master keeps prodding me with a stick. He just gives me some stale leftover food to eat at night. But the dog gets royal treatment. The master hugs him and leaves him home to rest. He gets juicy meat and milk for meals. I'll also

start doing what he does. Today when the master will come back I'll wag my tail, bray loudly as the dog barks and then rush to my master. Surely he'll pat me as he pats the dog."

That evening, when the potter came from some work, the donkey brayed loudly. He wagged his tail and rushed, raised his foot and licked the master's face as the dog did. But when the master saw the donkey braying and rushing towards him, he grew scared. He thought that the donkey was about to attack him so he beat up the donkey with a stout stick.

MORAL: Be happy as you are. Do not imitate others.

The Imitating Crow

Once there was an eagle who used to make high flights and then swoop to the ground on preys such as rabbits, squirrels or mice. There was a crow who used to admire the eagle's ability to do so.

One day a shepherd came to the place near the spot. He wandered off leaving his sheep to graze in the field. The eagle spotted a young lamb about a week old. So the eagle swooped down from the cliff, picked up the young lamb in his claws and flew off.

As usual the crow was observing the eagle's antics. He was impressed by the eagle's precision. He thought, "Both the eagle and I are birds. If he can get his prey by swooping so can I." With these thoughts, the crow flew to the sky as high up as he could. Then with great speed, he swooped towards the ground. But, like the eagle, the crow did not know how to glide and control his flight. So the crow struck the ground with great force. His neck and beak broke on contact with the ground. The crow died on the spot.

MORAL : Imitating others is not safe.

The Shepherd Boy's Lesson

A shepherd boy used to herd his flock to the grazing ground every day. The grazing ground was near a forest where many animals lived.

One day the shepherd boy felt mischievous. He decided to have some fun. He went to a high rock, stood on it and yelled, "Help! Wolf! Someone help me!"

Farmers working in the nearby fields heard his cries. They picked up stout sticks, axes and sickles and rushed to help the boy. When they reached there, the shepherd boy started laughing. "I made a fool of you, Ha... Ha... There is no wolf here. You can get back to work Ha ....Ha... Ha...!"

The farmers went back with a smile. The next day

the shepherd boy played the same trick. This time the farmers grew angry. "Don't lie like this, boy. You are wasting our time."

The third day by chance a wolf really came and started attacking his sheep. The boy kept calling for help but no one came to his rescue. They thought that he was lying once again. The wolf killed many of his sheep and went away. So the shepherd boy's trick had made him lose his sheep. He learnt never to lie in his life.

MORAL : No one believes a liar for once a liar always a liar.

The Woodcutter's Axe

A poor woodcutter was cutting a branch of a tree by a swift flowing river. By chance his axe slipped from his hands and fell into the river. As he had only that axe to work with, the woodcutter jumped into the river to retrieve it. But, alas ! He could not find it as the river water had swept it away.

The woodcutter grew sad and sat down by the riverside crying loudly. Hearing his cries, God Mercury, the messenger of Gods, appeared. He asked, "Why are you crying, young man ?"

"My Lord! My axe fell into the river. How will I cut wood to earn my living ?" the woodcutter cried.

God Mercury went into the river and came out with

a golden axe. He said, "Take this. I have found your axe."

"No, Sir. This is not mine. I can't take it," the woodcutter said.

God Mercury dived into the flowing waters once again. He came up with a silver axe this time. But the woodcutter refused to take that axe also. The third time God Mercury dived again and brought the woodcutter's iron axe in his hands. The woodcutter leapt with joy at the sight of his axe.

"Thank you for getting my axe back. Now I can get back to work."

God Mercury was very happy at the woodcutter's honesty. So he gifted the golden and silver axes to him.

MORAL : Honesty is the best policy.

The Capseller's Trick

One day a capseller was going round the village selling the caps. Soon the day grew hot. The capseller found a shady tree on the way. He stopped and sat under the tree. He took out his lunch and ate it. After that he decided to take a nap. He placed his bag full of colourful caps near his head and soon fell asleep.

When the capsellar was sleeping soundly, a troop of monkeys arrived under the tree. They saw the bag near the capseller's head and opened it curiously. They saw many colourful caps. They had seen men wearing them on their head. So true to their imitating nature, all of them took and wore the caps. Some wore the red ones and others the yellow ones. One picked up a black printed cap while another preferred one with orange and white embroidery. Then they ran up the tree under which the capseller slept.

A while later the capseller woke up. He found his bag of caps empty. He heard some noise and looked up the tree. The chattering monkeys were busy trying the caps. The capseller grew angry and showed the fists at them. The monkeys copied him. Then he stamped his feet on the ground in anger. The monkeys also stamped their feet on the branches. Now the capseller realized that the monkeys had copied him. So in mock anger the capseller took the cap from his head and threw it on the ground. The imitating monkeys copied him and did the same. The capseller gathered all the caps in his bag and fled away.

Moral: Sometimes common sense gets out of trouble.

The Proud Donkey

Once an idol maker made a large idol for Dussehra festival He was to deliver it to a rich merchant's house. As he could not carry the idol, he hired a donkey to carry it to the merchant's house. He placed the idol on the donkey's back and went on his way. On the way many people saw the idol of the goddess on the donkey's back. Out of religious ardour many of them bowed with folded hands. Some stopped just to admire the beauty of the craftsmanship.

The donkey thought that the people were bowing to him. He felt pride at the admiring looks he thought they were giving to him. So as he walked, the

foolish donkey started braying loudly in pride and pleasure. The idol maker said polite words to stop the donkey from braying. But the donkey brayed on. He started walking in a showy manner. The idol maker was afraid that the idol may fall off. In anger he took the stick and thrashed at the donkey's legs. The thrashing made the donkey realize to come to his sense. He forgot his false pride and walked properly without any proud antics.

MORAL : A fool only knows the rod's language.

The Unfaithful Friend

Ramu and Raju were childhood friends. Once they decided to go to the nearby town to look for work. On the way they had to pass through a thick forest. As they were walking through the forest, they saw a large bear approaching them. He looked fierce and hungry.

In fear Ramu ran and climbed up a tree. He forgot that his friend did not know how to climb a tree. So Ramu felt safe at the tree top and Raju's life was in danger. Raju kept calling Ramu for help but he did not help him climb the tree. Soon Raju saw the bear coming towards him. He did not know what to do. Suddenly an idea came into his mind. He had heard that bears do not eat a dead body. So he just lay on the ground and did not move. The bear came to Raju and sniffed him. Raju stopped breathing. The bear thought Raju was dead so he walked away.

When the bear had left, Ramu came down the tree. He asked Raju, "What was the bear whispering in your ear ?"

Raju replied, "He just warned me to stay away from unfaithful friends like you."

MORAL: A true friend never deserts in time of need.

The Clever Stork

A fox and a stork were fast friends. But even so the fox could not let go of her wicked nature. Once the fox decided to make fun of the stork. So she invited the stork for lunch. She prepared a delicious soup of chicken and corn. When the stork arrived for lunch, he was very hungry. The fox soon served two dishes of steaming soup. But the cunning fox had served the soup in flat dishes. The fox lapped up the soup quickly but the poor stork could not taste the soup. His long, thin beak could not taste a single drop of the soup. The stork realized that the fox had played a trick on him. He decided to take revenge.

After the lunch, the stork invited the fox for dinner to his own house. The fox was delighted. She started thinking about all the delicious dishes the stork would serve. As soon as the sun set, the fox dressed up and arrived at the stork's doorstep. She could smell the tasty fish soup being prepared in the kitchen. Soon the stork welcomed the fox in. The soup was served in narrow and long mouthed jar. The stork quickly dipped his beak into the jar and

drank up the soup. Alas ! All that the fox could do was smell the soup. The narrow mouth of the jar did not let her get at the soup in the jar. Now the fox understood how the stork had felt at the lunch time.

MORAL : Tit for tat

The Monkey Judge

Samy and Kitty were two cats. Once, while wandering in a garden, they found a piece of cake. Both of them leapt at it at once.

Samy mewed, "Hey, Kitty! This is my cake. I saw it first."

"No" exclaimed Kitty. "I picked it up first, so it is mine."

The argument soon heated up. A monkey sitting on a nearby tree was seeing all this. They asked him to judge who would get the cake.

The clever monkey took the cake and broke it into two. "You both can take equal halves of the cake."

But then he said, "Oh! This one is larger than the other. I'll bite off a piece to make them equal."

Then after eating a piece he said, "Now this one looks larger than the other. I must be just. Here I'll eat some more to make them equal."

Slowly he kept saying this and finished up the cake. The cats then realized that they had been fooled. Their fight had benefitted someone else and both of them had not tasted the cake at all.

> **MORAL : A third person gains when two people fight.**

The Kind Lion

A lion was taking a nap under a tree. A tiny mouse came out from his hole and climbed up the lion's back. The lion was disturbed. He woke up roaring and caught the mouse in his paw. The mouse squeaked, "Oh! I am sorry sir. I did not mean to disturb you. Please let me go. I'll surely help you whenever you need me in the future."

The lion laughed loudly, "What can a tiny, squeaky mouse do for me ? All right, I'll let you go."

So the lion let the mouse go and slept again.

Many days later some hunters spread a net to catch the lion. The lion got caught in it. As he roared in desperation, the mouse heard the lion and recognized his voice. He rushed to see what was wrong. He saw the lion caught in the net. The hunters were nowhere in sight. Quickly the mouse started nibbling at the strong ropes. After a while, he had chewed off the ropes and freed the lion. The lion hugged the tiny mouse thankfully. He now knew that the mouse had helped him as he had promised.

MORAL : Kindness is always repaid.

The Two Goats

Once a white goat and a black goat were crossing a river from the opposite banks. They were on a narrow bridge across the river. Only one man or animal could walk on it at one time. As the two goats met at the middle, the black goat said, "Hey ! Why are you blocking my path ? Go back and let me go on my way."

The white goat grew angry and said, "How dare you order me ? I'll not step back. Why don't you go back."

Soon the argument heated up. The two goats locked horns in anger. As they were fighting on the narrow bridge, they lost their balance and fell into the swift flowing river and both of them drowned.

MORAL : Anger creates problems not solutions.

The Golden Eggs

Once a poor farmer lived in a village. He had a goose. It had a magical quality. It used to lay a golden egg every morning. Everyday the farmer used to sell the golden egg in the market and get money. Soon he became a rich man. Once he had a greedy idea. He thought, "I have become rich with one golden egg that the goose lays every day. It must be having a lot of them in its stomach. I'll cut open its stomach and get all the golden eggs at once."

With such wicked thought, the farmer picked up a large knife and went to the barn. He cut the goose's stomach wide open. But he found no golden eggs in it. The goose had died and left the farmer feeling miserable for his evil deed.

MORAL : Greed breeds misfortunes.

The Dog in the Stream

One day a kind butcher gave a large piece of bone to a hungry dog. The dog picked the bone in his mouth and went across the stream because he wanted to eat it at a lonely place. As he was walking over the bridge, he looked into the stream. He saw a dog with a large piece of bone in his mouth. He was not aware that it was his own reflection. He thought that this is an another dog with a piece of bone. "Oh ! What a juicy bone this dog has ! If I can get this bone, I will have two bones to eat. I am so hungry. I'll bark loudly to frighten the dog away. He'll run away leaving the bone behind and I'll take it for myself."

With such thoughts the dog barked loudly. There was no reply to his barking but only a loud splash. The piece of bone from his mouth fell into the stream and the dog became sad and remained hungry.

> **MORAL : Be contented with what you have.**

The Lazy Grasshopper

It was winter season. There were colours and beauty all around. Birds and animals were happy. They had fine weather to enjoy and lot of food to eat.

One day a grasshopper was happily sitting on a leaf and humming a melodious tune. He was observing some ants collecting eatables for their hard days. Each of them was busy in carrying the grains to their homes and storing them. Making fun of them, grasshopper said to one of them, "Why are you busy working ? Enjoy these beautiful winter days. Eat well and make merry !"

The ant said, "These are winter days. It is not known when the snow will fall .We are storing the food for that time. After snowfall we won't get any food."

"Ha ! What a foolish thing to do ! Worrying about the future !" Saying so, the grasshopper lazed in the sun.

By the middle of the winter season the trees were bare of leaves. Then began the snowfall. Insects went underground and the birds flew to the south. Animals were not around. The grasshopper found nothing to eat as the snow had covered the ground. No one came out due to the cold. The grasshopper went to the ant and asked for some food. The ant said, "We are happy in our cozy homes with a lot of food. We are reaping rewards of our hard work in the past. You were happy being lazy and singing in the sun. Why don't you sing now ? Go away we don't entertain lazy creatures like you !"

MORAL : Saving for the future is best planning.

Dinner in the Town

A country mouse had a town mouse as his cousin. Once the town mouse went to meet the country mouse. The country mouse served berries, roots, grains and nuts to his cousin. But the town mouse made a face and said, "Oh ! Such a boring lunch. It tastes no good. Come to town with me and I'll give you a lavish dinner."

The country mouse went with the town mouse. He lived in a hole in a wall of a house in a dark street. The town mouse really served a lavish dinner. There were cheese, jam, bread, honey, dates, fig and dry fruits. The town mouse sat down to enjoy dinner. But, after every bite, the town mouse asked his cousin to nibble noiselessly. He said, "If we nibble loudly or talk loudly, the cat wandering around will come to get us."

After a while the cat's mews were heard nearby. Throughout dinner, the town mouse was afraid that the cat would get them. After the dinner, the country mouse said, "Cousin, I am going back to the field in the countryside. At least I can enjoy my simple food in the fresh air and without fear of a cat."

MORAL : Riches are not always pleasure-giving.

The Race

Once a hare and a tortoise got into an argument about their speeds. The hare challenged the tortoise that whatever may happen but the fast hare would always win the race. But the tortoise did not agree. So to prove that the hare was faster than the slow moving tortoise, a race was held.

On the appointed day, the animals of the forests gathered at the starting and finish points of the race. The lion was to be the judge. Soon the giraffe blew the whistle and the race began. The fast hopping hare ran off at great speed. The slow tortoise had barely taken a step by then. Soon the hare got near a tree from where he could see the finishing line. He was tired after the run, so he thought, "Let me rest a while. The slow tortoise will take a long time to reach here. As soon as I see him here, I'll just run and reach the finishing line." With these thoughts, the hare fell asleep.

The slow tortoise kept crawling, never waiting to rest. Walking slowly and continuously, he soon reached the finishing line. The amazed forest

animals clapped and shouted in joy. The hare heard the noise and woke up. He was shocked to see the tortoise at the finishing line. The lion was crowning him as the winner.

MORAL : Slow and steady wins the race.

The Sour Grapes

Once a fox was wandering around in search of food. She came to the edge of the woodland where she lived. She saw that a vineyard was nearby. She went there and saw ripe juicy grapes hanging there. The fox jumped up to reach them but could not. She gathered courage and jumped again with her full strength but still could not reach the grapes. Yet she kept trying to reach the grapes by jumping again and again. Soon she started sweating and grew tired. She stopped and took a deep breath.

Then she sighed and said, "Oh ! Why try so hard for such sour grapes ? Let them be."

With such thoughts the fox went back to the woodland.

MORAL : One must accept defeat sportingly.

The Thirsty Crow

On a hot summer afternoon a crow was flying around in search of water. He was feeling very thirsty. He flew all over the forest but got no water there. The heat was overbearing and the streams and ponds of the forests had dried up. Then he crossed over into a nearby village. There he saw an old hut. An old earthern pot was lying in its courtyard. The crow flew down to investigate. Luckily the pot had some water. But it was very little and at the bottom of the pot. The crow had found this water after a long time. He was determined to drink and quench his thirst. But the beak of the crow could not reach the water. So he became sad.

The crow grew thoughtful. He looked around to find a way to reach the water at the bottom of the pot. He saw some pebbles lying nearby. Seeing the pebbles, the crow had an idea. He picked up the pebbles in his beak one by one and dropped them in to the pot. Gradually, the water level in the pot rose up to the rim of the pot. The crow drank the water to his full and flew away.

MORAL : Determination achieves all.

The King's Lesson

Once a battle was being fought near a mountain. The battle was being fought between two kings. One had a large, well-equipped army and the other had a small army. Soon the king with the smaller army began to lose his men. Seeing this, the king lost all hope and courage. He was very tired and had many injuries, too. He had no hope of winning the battle now. So he ran away from the battle-field and reached a mountainous forest. He found a cave in the mountain and went inside it. He lied down to rest.

As he lay there looking at the cave wall, he saw a spider. The spider was climbing up to its web. When it was about to reach its web, it felt a jerk and fell down. It made the next attempt, but got the same result. The king was watching the spider's attempts. Each time it tried, the thread would break and it would fall to the ground. The spider tried several times but could not reach its web. At last it pulled the thread across and soon reached its web. The king had observed all this. He thought, "This spider is such a tiny creature but it was firmly determined to complete its task. It did not lose hope or give up when it failed. I must learn a lesson from this spider that never to give up. I'll go and fight the large army at all odds. I'll try my best."

With these positive thoughts, the king went back to the battle-field. He encouraged his small army to keep fighting and he, too, fought hard. At last the king and his small army won the battle and all of them rejoiced.

MORAL : **Failures must not hold you back.**
Take them as challenges.

The Salt-seller's Donkey

A donkey worked for a salt-seller. The salt-seller would load the salt sacks on the donkey's back and take it to the town market every day.

One day as the salt-seller and the donkey were crossing the river between their village and the town, the donkey slipped and fell into the water. Soon the salt of the sacks dissolved in the river-water. The donkey felt its burden lightened. The salt had been wasted. As there was no salt to be sold, the salt-seller turned back for the village. That day they did not go to town and so the donkey had a rest.

Next morning as the salt-seller and the donkey were crossing the river, the donkey slipped and fell again. But this time the donkey had done it knowingly. The salt-seller realized what the donkey was upto. He did not do anything. He went back home as the day before. The donkey felt glad that its plan had worked.

The next day, too, the donkey intended to do the same. But the salt-seller had other plans. As every morning the salt-seller loaded the sacks on the donkey's back. The donkey felt the heavy sacks on his back. The only difference was that the salt-seller had put sacks full of bales of cotton on the donkey's back. As they left for the town market, they came to the bridge once again. The donkey thought of its plan once again. It acted as if it had lost its balance and slipped into the river-water. But the bales of cotton in the sacks did not dissolve as salt did. Instead the bales soaked in the water and the sacks grew heavier. The weight pulled down the donkey into the water. Its struggles were observed by the salt-seller with a smile. Then the salt-seller helped the donkey come out of the river-

water. It had nearly drowned. The donkey understood that the salt-seller had played a trick to teach him a lesson. The donkey never tried to play the same trick ever again.

MORAL : Over confidence may spell doom.

The Wolf's Death

A wolf had found out a farm near the jungle. Many sheep and cattle were kept there in sheds and pens. He tried many times to get a sheep to eat but the shepherd's servants never let him get to the sheep.

One day the wolf found a sheep-skin. So the wolf thought of a plan. That evening the wolf covered himself in the sheep-skin. Then he stealthily entered the sheeps' pen. He was sure that night he would have a fat sheep for dinner.

That evening the shepherd had some guests for dinner. He asked his cook to fetch a sheep from the pen and cook it for dinner. The cook went into the pen. As it was late in the evening, it was dark in the pen. The cook could not see clearly. He just picked the wolf in the sheep-skin and cut its head in the dark.

Thus, the wolf had met a sorry end. That night, the shepherd's guests ate a delicious dinner little realizing that they were having the poor wolf's meat.

MORAL : Bad intentions meet bad ends.

The Pot's Tale

A poor woman had a copper pot and an earthen pot in her kitchen. The copper pot was proud of its shine and strength and always looked down on the earthen pot.

Once there was a flood in the village. The flood water entered the poor woman's house. All the house articles were swept away in the flood. By chance, the two pots floated out together. They soon were being swept away in the swift waters. When the copper pot saw the earthen pot being swept away, he said, "Why are you there ? Come near me. You are made of mud and will not be saved. If you will be near me, you'll be safe and protected."

The earthen pot smiled politely and said, "Thank you, my friend, but I won't come near you at all. As you said I am made of mud so I am weak and delicate. If I'll be near to you and a wave hits you then we'll crash into each other, and I'll break into many bits. I'd rather be alone and safe. Please don't come near me."

> **MORAL : Over powerful people often spell trouble.**

The Sun's Challenge

One day a heated argument took place between the sun and the wind. Each claimed that it was stronger than the other. So they set a challenge to prove which one was the stronger one.

They saw a man walking by. He was wearing a coat. The sun and the wind decided that whosoever would make the man take off the coat would be accepted as the stronger one.

The wind decided to try first. So he began to blow very hard. As the wind blew, the man felt cold. So he drew the coat closer to his body. The wind blew harder and the man hugged the coat tighter. At last wind grew tired and gave up.

Now it was the sun's chance. The sun started shining with all his glory. The man felt the slight warmth of the sun. The coat's buttons were now open. The sun shined harder. The man took his coat off and hung it on his shoulder. The sun kept shining harder. The man could not take the heat any longer. So he looked for a shady tree and sat down under it.

Thus the sun had made the man take off his coat and he was declared the stronger one.

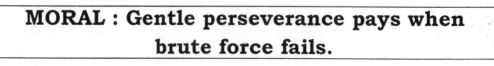

MORAL : Gentle perseverance pays when
brute force fails.

The Farmer's Sons

A farmer had four, young and hardworking sons. But everyday they would quarrel due to some reason or the other. Their quarrels would upset the farmer. He wanted to see them happy all the time.

One day the farmer thought of an idea. He called his four sons into his bed room. A bundle of sticks was lying in a corner. He called his elder son and said, "Son, go and get the bundle of sticks." The son picked up the bundle. Then the farmer said, "Son, now use all your strength to break these sticks without opening the bundle."

The son agreed. He tried hard to break the bundle but none of the sticks broke. Then the farmer asked each of his son to try their best to break the sticks but none of them succeeded.

Then the farmer asked them to untie the bundle of sticks and said, "Now pick one stick each and try to break it."

Each of the four sons easily broke the sticks into two in a single jerk.

Then the farmer addressed his sons, "Sons, did you see how all your strength could not break the bundle of sticks ? But all of you broke the single stick very easily. So is the way with all of you. If you

stay together lovingly, without quarrelling, you'll be strong. No one can harm our family. If each of you think separately and quarrel with each other, you'll be weak. Then anyone can easily break our family."

The sons understood what their father was telling them. From that day the brothers lived an united and loving life.

MORAL : Union is strength.

The Goat and the Monkey

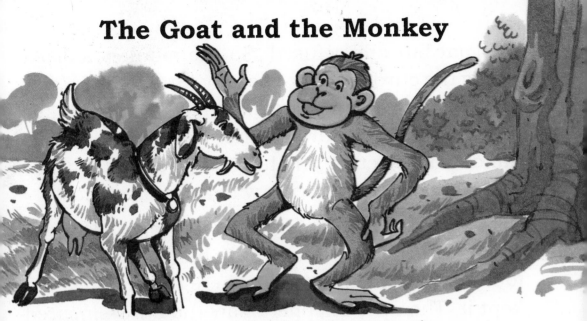

A shepherd used to take his sheep to the pasture daily. He used to take his pets, a monkey and a goat with him. In the pasture, the shepherd used to tie the goat to a tree. The monkey would be allowed to roam around freely. The naughty monkey used to take advantage of this. He used to tease the goat by pulling its tail or tickling her. The goat was helpless as she was tied to the tree.

One day, as usual, the shepherd left his pets and went off with the sheep. The restless monkey started teasing the goat and said, "I am feeling hungry. Let me check what the master has in his lunch-box. We'll both share the food."

The goat shook her head and said, "No ! No ! I won't eat it. You must also not touch the master's lunch-box."

But the monkey did not listen to the goat. He took the shepherd's lunch-box and opened it. There was tasty curd and rice in it. The monkey offered it to the goat but she refused. So the monkey started eating the curd and rice speedily. Suddenly he saw the shepherd coming at a distance. So the monkey quickly ate up the curd and rice and then wiped his hands full of curd on the goat's face. Then the monkey settled in a corner with an innocent look.

Soon the shepherd arrived at the spot. He was feeling hungry. He looked for his lunch-box. He found it lying near the goat where the monkey had kept it. Then the shepherd saw the curd-smeared mouth of the goat. He assumed that the goat had eaten up his lunch. So the goat got a sound beating from his master.

MORAL : Bad company always spells trouble.

Fatherly Love

A young farmer named Somu used to work hard in his field. He would start working at sunrise and went on till sunset. He stopped only for

lunch. At times he would not even care for the hot sun beating down his back at noon.

Somu's father was an old man. He had given the field to his son. He could not work or help him due to old age. But he used to be worried for Somu. Whenever he saw Somu working and sweating under the sun, he would say. "Son, why don't you rest a while ? Come in the shade and have some water."

But Somu would say, "Father, let me work now. If I start taking rest, I'll feel lazy."

Somu did not listen and his father was afraid that his son would fall ill this way. Another day when he

complained, Somu said, "Father, I am a strong young man. Stop caring for me as if I was a baby."

Somu's father smiled and said, "Wait till you have your own child. You'll understand what I go through seeing you toiling in the sun."

A few months later, Somu got married. A year later Somu became the father of a healthy and beautiful baby boy. Even then Somu's father had not stopped fussing over his son.

One summer afternoon, Somu was working in the field as usual. He was sweating in the sun. As usual, his father asked him to rest but Somu did not relent. Just then an idea occurred to Somu's father. He went into the hut and came out with his grandson in his arms. He placed the baby in the corner of the field. Soon the baby felt uncomfortable and hot under the sun. Soon he started crying loudly. The baby's cries caught Somu's attention. He ran and picked the baby in his arms. Somu took the baby under a shady peepal tree. Then he turned to his father and said, "Father, what is this ? I didn't expect you to act so foolishly. How could you let my innocent son lie under the hot sun."

"Son", Somu's father smiled. "I know what you are feeling. I used to feel the same love and concern seeing you working in the field under the sun without rest. You never paid attention to my caring words. This was the only way I could make you realize my fatherly love for you."

Somu felt that he had been hurting his father's feelings for so long. From that day, he did as his father wanted.

> **MORAL : The parents' love does not lessen even when the child grows up.**

The Sage's Parrot

One day a traveller was passing through a jungle. He felt very tired. He decided to rest a while under a peepal tree. Soon he got a shady tree and settled under it for a nap.

"I'll get you ! Just wait ! I'll kill you or catch you for sure."

A harsh screechy voice scared the traveller. He got up and looked around. He saw a parrot in the leafy branches of the tree.

"I'll kill you or catch you for sure !" the parrot screeched again.

The traveller got up and walked a few steps. He saw another shady tree and sat down to rest.

"Welcome sir ! Will you have some water or fruits ?

Please relax."

A sweet voice greeted the traveller. As the traveller looked to find the source of the voice, he saw another parrot. It was almost exactly like the parrot he had seen before. Suddenly the parrot took flight. The traveller was surprised. How could such same looking parrots speak so differently ? He decided to follow the flying parrot.

The parrot flew on and the traveller followed it. A few minutes later, the parrot flew into a large ashram. The traveller entered the hut in the ashram. A sage sat there in deep meditation.

"Welcome, sir ! Will you have some water or fruits? Please relax."

The parrot repeated once more. At the parrot's

voice, the sage opened his eyes.

"Yes ! What can I do for you ?" the sage addressed the traveller.

"Sir, I followed this sweet-talking parrot to the ashram. In the jungle, I saw another such parrot who spoke rather harshly. Will you clear this confusion I have ?"

The sage smiled and said, " A she parrot had given birth to two young ones. One of the young parrots was caught by a hunter. The other young parrot fell

down from the tree. It was injured. I brought it up in my ashram. It has grown up hearing my pupils' polite words, so it merely repeats that, and the parrot caught by the hunter has learnt his rude language. So even though they have the same mother, the parrots are different in behaviour."

MORAL : A person develops his character influenced by his environs not by his birth.

The Milkman's Lesson

Once there lived a dishonest milkman. He used to mix water in the milk and would sell it to his customers.

One day the milkman had sold all his milk. After selling the milk, he had a heavy purse full of coins. He was feeling tired. He saw a shady tree beside a well and went to take rest under it. The breeze was blowing gently. So within a few minutes he slept deeply.

The milkman woke up after an hour or so. He heard the jingling of coins. He looked up. A monkey had taken the milkman's purse of coins and climbed up the tree. The monkey thought the purse had something to eat. The monkey took a coin out of the purse and bit it but nothing happened. The monkey threw the coin down in anger.

Then the monkey took out another coin from the purse, bit it and threw it down. This way the monkey threw all the coins down one by one.

Some coins fell down on the ground and some into the well. When the purse was empty the monkey threw it to the ground.

The milkman had to watch it helplessly. The milkman pick up his empty bag, collected the coins fell on the ground and counted them. His purse had held a hundred coins. Now he had only fifty of them. Thus, he had half the money that was truly his earning. The other fifty coins were in the water where they belonged as he had put water in the milk to sell to the customers.

MORAL : Dishonesty is always punished.

Money's Worth

Once a couple had a son after nearly ten years of marriage. They brought him up lovingly. They fulfilled all their son's wishes. They gave him whatever he asked for.

Years passed and their son grew into a young man but he had become a spoilt brat. His father tried hard to change the habits of the son, but the son merely went around spending his father's hard earned money.

One day his father called him and said, "Son, you've been wasting money all these years. After all I'll leave all the money and property for you. But now if you want me to do that, then you will have to prove to me that you can earn money on your own, too."

The young man accepted the challenge. He went to look for a job. After trying many times, he finally found a job. He was to load and unload sacks of grains from vehicles into the godowns. He worked hard carrying the sacks on his back and on his head. At the end of the day, he got merely twenty rupees.

But he was happy to get his hard earned money. He took the twenty-rupee note home and gave it to his father. His father didn't say a word. He went and threw the note in the well behind their house. The young man did not protest though he was surprised. The next day he earned twenty rupees again and handed them to his father. His father threw the money into the well once again. This happened everyday for a week. Then one day the son grew very angry. He said, "Father, I work hard the whole day to earn that twenty rupees and you just throw it in the well. If only you know how precious that money is."

The young man's father smiled, patted his back and said, "Son, now do you know how I felt all these years when you wasted my hard earned money ?"

The son realized his mistake and never wasted any money.

MORAL : One learns the value of money only when one earns it.

The Miserly Merchant

Once a miserly merchant lost his purse. It had a hundred gold coins. He went to the village headman and lodged a complaint about it. The headman advised that if a reward for the finder would be announced, the purse would be looked for by all. The miserly merchant accepted this proposal half heartedly as there was no other way. So the village headman announced a reward of ten gold coins for the one who finds the purse.

A poor farmer found the purse with a hundred gold coins. He took the purse, went to the merchant's mansion and handed it over to him. The merchant felt very happy that his gold coins had been found. He thanked the farmer and shut the door. The farmer thought that the merchant had gone in to get the ten gold coins as reward. He waited for nearly fifteen minutes then he knocked at the door. When the merchant opened the door, he said, "Sir, what about the reward that had been announced ?"

"What reward ? I counted the gold coins when I was

inside. There were hundred and ten coins when I lost the purse. Now there are only a hundred which means you've already taken the money. Now don't bother me, Just leave !"

With these words, the merchant shut the door. The

poor man rushed to the village headman and told him what had occurred. The village headman sent for the merchant and asked him to bring the purse along. On the merchant's arrival. the village headman took the purse and heard what the merchant had to say. After hearing both the men, the village headman said to the merchant, "You say that your purse had a hundred and ten gold coins. But this small purse can hold only a hundred gold coins at one time. So I guess this purse is not yours at all. The farmer has wrongly taken you as its owner. Since the real owner is not present here, so I give this purse full of a hundred gold coins to him as a reward for his honesty."

The farmer humbly and happily accepted his reward. The miserly merchant went home without any gold coins.

MORAL : Cheaters are always losers.

The Contented Man

A king had the habit of going round his kingdom enquiring about the welfare of his people. But every time he went out, he always found that the people had some woe or worry troubling them. None of them ever seemed to be happy or contented. On one such occasion the king exclaimed, "All these times, I have never found a happy person in my kingdom. Is there no one in my kingdom who is fully content with his life ?"

With such thoughts the king rode on his horse and passed by a village. He saw a very old man digging in a field. The old man was working hard, not heeding the hot sunshine. He was so busy in his work that he was not even aware of the king's arrival. The king approached the old man and said, "Who are you, Baba ? What are you doing in the hot sun ?"

The old man was surprised to see the king. He said, "Your Majesty, I am digging the field to plant some mango trees."

"After how many days will these trees give the fruits ?" asked the king.

"After about five years," replied the old man.

"Then what's the use of this ?" the king said. "Don't mind, I mean you are an old man now. The mango trees will take five years to give you its fruits. Do you think you will be alive till it starts giving the fruits."

The old man turned to the king with a smile and said, "Your Majesty, I know this very well. I am not planting these trees to get their fruits for myself. It's for my sons and grandsons to enjoy. If my ancestors had thought the same way then today I would not have enjoyed the fruits of the mango trees growing here. I have taken these seeds from the trees sown by my ancestors." The king was pleased to have found a happy and contented man who had taught him a great lesson, too.

MORAL : Selfless giving makes a heart content.

The Dead Crocodile

Once there lived a crocodile in a lake full of fish. There lived a crab, too, in the same lake. The crocodile and the crab were good friends. They used to help each other to catch their preys.

One day the crocodile said, "Dear Crab, I am fed up of tasting fish everyday. No animals come to drink water in the lake anymore. They fear that I'll attack them. But I want to have something other than fish."

"Oh yes, my friend ! I also feel the same," said the crab. "Let me think and I'll make a plan to get some other animal for lunch today."

The crab grew thoughtful. Then he said, "I have an idea. You go and lie there under the tree. Don't move at all. I'll go and tell the animals in the jungle not to fear anymore. I'll ask them to come to the lake to drink water fearlessly as you are dead. I'll ask them to come near and check for themselves. As soon as they come close to you, you can catch them."

The crocodile was impressed by the crab's plan. He

promptly went and lay under the tree. The crab left for the jungle. There he saw a young healthy jackal. He went to the jackal and said, "Dear Jackal, I have some good news for you. The crocodile of the lake is dead. You and your other jungle friends can come to the lake to quench your thirst. I want you to come and see for yourself that the crocodile is dead. He is lying under a tree by the lake."

The jackal was also a wise one. He thought he should check as the crab said. But, in his mind the jackal had his suspicions. The jackal followed the crab to the tree. From a safe distance, the jackal saw the crocodile lying motionless under a tree. Then the jackal thought of playing a trick to confirm if the crocodile was truly dead. So in a loud

voice, which the crocodile could hear from a distance, the jackal said to the crab, "Friend, are you sure the crocodile is dead ? Did you see its tail well ? A wise owl once told me that a dead crocodile's tail keeps moving even after its death."

The foolish crocodile heard the jackal's words and promptly shook his tail real hard. Now the jackal was sure that the crocodile was alive. So he called loudly, "Oh ! Don't you know that dead things don't move at all ! Now I'll tell all the other animals about your foolish plan."

With these words the jackal ran away and the foolish crocodile had to eat fish again.

MORAL : Appearance can be deceptive.

The White Crow

One day a crow was flying over a village. He came down and sat on a wall to look for food. Clouds had gathered in the sky and suddenly a thunder clap sounded in the sky. This startled the crow. He slipped and fell off the wall. The wall  surrounded the courtyard of a painter's house. The crow had fallen into a tub full of white lime. He struggled out with difficulty and flew to a nearby

pond, As he sat there on the edge of the pond, he looked into the water. He saw a white crow in the water. He was taken aback. Then he realized it was his own reflection. The white lime had turned him white from beak to tail.

The crow flew back to the jungle and to the

tree where he lived. On the way he thought of a plan. When he reached the jungle he started cawing loudly. This attracted the other crows' attention. They all observed a bird white in colour but cawing just like them. They followed the bird to the tree. There the white crow said, "Friends, I have a message from the Jungle God. He has appointed me to be your king. From today onwards, you all must serve me and obey all my commands."

The crows were surprised to see a white crow, so they believed all that the white crow said. Thus, the white crow became the king. He enjoyed it when the other crows bowed to him and obeyed his orders. Soon the white crow became full of pride.

One day it rained very heavily. All the crows huddled in the thick leafy branches of a large

banyan tree. The white crow was also among them. But the branches could not keep all the raindrops away. Some birds were getting wet. The white crow was also getting wet due to the rain. Suddenly some crows started staring at the white crow in surprise. Some were looking shocked and others were looking angry. Actually the raindrops had started washing off the white lime from the white crow's body. Streaks of black colour were showing but the white crow was unaware of this. Soon all the white lime got washed away and the white crow sat exposed as an ordinary black crow. All the crows cawed in anger and attacked the cheat. The pretender king had to flee the jungle to save his life.

MORAL : Don't try to be, what you are not.

The Horse-Riders

One day a farmer and his son went to a city to buy a horse. They paid a heavy amount and bought a handsome black horse. Then they both sat on horse back and rode on to their village.

On the way a group of people saw them. One of them commented, "Oh ! What a fine horse. The poor beast is looking so sad. I think it cannot bear the load of both the men on its back."

Hearing this, the farmer got off the horse's back and started walking beside the horse. The son kept riding the horse. As they went on, they passed through a market. Many people saw the young man on horse back. A shopkeeper said, "Shame on this young man ! He is young and fit yet he rides the horse while the old man is walking."

This comment upset the farmer's son. He got down and let his father ride the horse. They kept going to their village. On the way, they had to pass a lake. Some women were washing clothes by the lake side. One of them said, "Oh ! What a cruel old man ! He is making that young boy walk in the sun. He does not have any feelings for him at all."

Hearing this, the old man got down. Both the father and son were angry hearing the comments made by the people. They had now come to a bridge across a river. They picked up the horse and then threw it into the fast-flowing current of the river. The horse drowned. Then the farmer smiled and

said, "That's the end of it ! I was fed up listening to so many peoples' comments. It was all because of this horse. Now the horse is dead and we don't need to listen to anyone."

Then the farmer and the son went home happily. They were foolish not to realize their loss.

MORAL : Don't go by others' opinions. Do as you think best.

The True Mother

Once two women went to King Solomon for justice. Both of them were claiming that the other had stolen her baby. The baby in one's lap was upset and was crying loudly. In the confusion, King Solomon was finding it difficult to judge. One of the women said, "Your Majesty, your justice is praised far and wide. Please hand over the baby to me. I cannot live without this baby."

"No, Your Majesty," the second woman said. "She is lying. This baby is mine. She has made some plan to take away my baby."

The argument made by both the women were felt true. It became very difficult to judge who the real mother of the baby was. Thinking for a few seconds, King Solomon got an idea. He said, to his guards, "It is a very difficult case. To end this quarrel and to make both the women contended, cut the baby

into two equal parts and give one part to each." "No, Your Majesty! Please don't do it," the first woman cried out with folded hands. " I have no right on this baby. She is its real mother. Let her keep the baby."

At this King Solomon smiled and said to her, "You can take your baby home. This lying woman will be punished."

Then King Solomon said, "She is the real mother of this baby. A real mother can never bear to let her baby fall in any kind of difficulty. That is why she is denying the baby to be her own." Then to the guards , King Solomon said, " Now guards, put the other woman in prison for lying and stealing a baby."

MORAL : There is no love like a mother's love

The Son's Lesson

Once a poor couple had a son. After a few years, the mother of the child died. The father worked hard day and night to give the best food and clothing to his only son. He earned a lot of money and provided the best schooling and college education to his son.

Years passed by and the boy grew up into a handsome young man. He had no bad habits and was very well behaved. But in his heart, he felt ashamed of his old and poor father who had lived in a village. Soon the young man married a beautiful city girl from a very wealthy family. As there was no one to look after the old father, his poor father moved into their city mansion. But, as the young man was ashamed of his father, he gave him a shed in the backyard to live in. He gave him some old clothes to wear. He never went to meet his father. The servants used to give some leftovers to him for lunch and dinner.

A few years later, the young man had a son. As the boy grew up, he used to observe his father treating the old man shabbily. He used to feel bad about it. He had great love and sympathy for his grandfather.

Once on a cold night, the little boy saw his grandfather shivering in the open shed. So he picked up his father's warm blanket to give to his grandfather. Just then his father came and said, "Where are you taking my blanket ?"

"Father, Grandfather is feeling cold. I'll give the blanket to him."

At this the boy's father took an old torn blanket from the store room and gave it to the boy. He said, "Go and give this old blanket to the old man. That is

enough for him."

The little boy took the old blanket and gave it to his grandfather but he didn't like it. He went back to his room and cut his father's new blanket with a scissor. He took some of his father's clothes and tore them. He put all of them together. His father came to him and asked, "Why have you torn my clothes and blanket ?"

The boy said, "I am keeping them for your old age. When I grow up I will give these clothes to you like you give torn clothes to the grandfather."

Hearing this, the young man and his wife were taken aback. They felt sorry and realized their mistake in how they had treated the old man. They went to the old man and apologised. After that they kept him in comfort in the mansion where they lived.

MORAL : As you sow, so shall you reap.

The Astrologer's Prediction

A king was very fond of meeting astrologers to know about his future. Many astrologers were invited to his court. He used to give them food and gifts after hearing favourable predictions.

One day a learned astrologer visited the king. As usual, the astrologer was given a warm welcome. Then the astrologer asked to read the king's palm. After a thoughtful study, the astrologer declared, "Your Majesty, I am sad to say that you won't live for long. You will breathe your last in a few days, so you must be careful."

Hearing these words, the king got very angry. He

called his guards and said, "Take this astrologer with you and hang him. I don't want to see his face. Tell all the people to come and see him being hanged after seven days."

"Your Majesty," the astrologer said. "Please take back your words."

"Why ?" asked the king. "Because, according to what I read in your hand, you will die three days before my death," the astrologer answered.

At this the king released the astrologer. Thus, the clever astrologer got away with his quick thought plan.

MORAL : Cleverness is at times better than all the learning.

A Riddle to Solve

Once an intelligent but poor farmer lived in a village. He used to help the people with his wise advice.

One day the king was passing through the village. He saw the farmer and called him. The king asked, "How much money do you earn ? How do you spend it ?"

At this the wise farmer replied, "Your Majesty, I earn one rupee each day. I eat the first quarter of it. I lend the second quarter. I pay back the third quarter and I throw away the fourth quarter."

"Will you explain that to me in detail," the king asked.

"Your Majesty, I spend the first quarter on food for my wife and myself, so I eat it. The money spent on my children is like insuring my future. They will take care of me in old age, so I lend the second quarter. The third quarter I pay back by spending on my parents who brought me up. The last quarter I throw away I give it as alms to the poor."

Hearing this clever reply, the king said, "Now I order you never to tell the answer of this riddle to anyone till you have seen my face a hundred times."

The farmer promised so and the king went back to his palace. The next day he posed the same riddle to his ministers in the royal court. No one could solve the riddle. So the king gave three days to the ministers to find the answer.

A minister had learnt that the king had met a wise farmer in a village. So he guessed the answer may be found with the farmer. The minister went to the village to search for the farmer. The minister found the farmer but the farmer refused to tell the answer due to the promise he had made. Then the minister took a hundred coins from his purse and gave it to the farmer. Every coin had the king's face engraved on it. The farmer counted them, looking at each coin closely and then told the minister the answer to the riddle.

Next day the minister gave the answer to the riddle in court. The king then enquired and found that the farmer had revealed the answer. He grew very angry and rode to meet the farmer in the village. He angrily scolded the farmer for having broken the promise he had made. At this, the farmer said, "Your Majesty, I did not break the promise. I saw your face a hundred times before I gave the answer."

"How dare you lie to me ? I did not come to meet you after that one meeting. How did you see my face a hundred times ?"

"Your Majesty, here are the coins the minister gave to me. These are hundred coins and each of these has your face imprinted on it."

The king was very pleased and impressed by the farmer's words. He gave him many more gifts and gold coins.

MORAL : Wisdom does not come with riches.

The Helpful Dove

There once lived a dove on a tree. A fat red hen living in a nearby farmyard was the dove's best friend. They used to meet every evening to share jokes and talk about others.

One day a hungry fox entered the farmyard. She went in stealthily and caught the red hen. The fox put the hen in a sack and walked off. The hen started cackling loudly in protest. The dove sitting on a tree branch had seen what had happened. So she quickly thought of an idea to save her friend.

The dove flew far ahead of the fox. She went and lay down on the path on which the fox was walking. She lay motionless as if she was dead. As the fox came near the dead dove, she thought "Wow! What a lucky day it is today. I have a juicy red hen in my sack and now I see a dead dove lying on the path. I'll pick the dove, too. Then I'll have a very juicy, delicious lunch in the afternoon."

With these thoughts the fox put the sack down by the path. The hen realized that the fox had put down the sack and struggled to get out. The fox approached the 'dead' dove but just as she reached out her hands to get the dove, the 'dead' dove flew off. The fox stepped back in surprise. Then she thought, "Let her go. I still have the hen in my sack for lunch."

Meanwhile the hen had got out of the sack. She had placed a large heavy piece of stone in the sack. Then she went and hid behind a bush. The fox returned, picked up the sack and went home. At home when she opened the sack, she was shocked to see that the hen had turned into a large piece of stone.

The dove and hen were rejoicing on the success of the dove's plan.

MORAL : A bird in hand is better than two in
the bush.

The Proud Elephant

Once a large, proud elephant was passing through a forest. He was not paying attention to any other animals on the way. As he walked on, he was about to trample down an anthill with his heavy legs. The ants cried out, "Hey ! Look, where you are stepping ? You were about to break our anthill. Don't you have any manners at all ?"

The proud elephant laughed aloud and said, "Look,

who is talking ! You tiny ants have a lot of guts to talk to me this way. You tiny creatures are of no use. I wonder why you were created. You are so small and weak that I can blow you and your home in one whiff from my trunk."

The insulting comments angered the ants. They all decided to teach the elephant a lesson. So they got together and climbed up the elephant's legs and started biting him hard. But the elephant's thick skin did not let him feel the bites.

A young clever ant was watching all this from the anthill. He made a plan. He went and told the other ants, "Go and attack his eyes. They are sensitive. I'll get into his ears."

The ants rushed to the elephant's eyes. The young ant got into one of the ears of the elephant. As the ants started biting, the elephant grew restless. He tried hard but there was no way he could get the

ants out of his eyes. He roamed around blindly trumpeting in pain. The ant in his ear bit the soft skin inside the ear. The elephant could not get at the tiny ant. In desperation the elephant rubbed its head against the tree. The ant in his ear bit hard and said. "Now you know how strong we tiny creature may be."

Within a few minutes the blind elephant crashed into a huge tree and fell down unconscious. The ants exclaimed, "See how the mighty have fallen !"

MORAL : Might is not always right.

For the Good of All

One day a king was standing in the balcony of his palace. It was a windy and cool evening. As the wind started getting wilder, the king went to the door to get back into his

chamber. Just then a strong wind blew. The doors to the chamber shut with a loud bang. As the king had placed his hand on the door to get in, his finger caught between the two doors. The king's finger was cut. He cried out in pain.

Hearing his cries, the guards and the king's wise prime minister arrived on the scene immediately. Seeing that the king's finger was cut, the guards said some sympathetic words but the prime minister said, "Whatever happens, happens for the good."

Hearing these unconsoling words, the king lost his temper. He said, "Guards, go and put him in prison." So the prime minister was imprisoned. The king appointed a new prime minister.

A few weeks later, the king, the prime minister and

some servants went on a hunting trip. In the jungle, some dacoits caught the king along with his prime minister and servants. They were looking for men to be sacrificed in the name of their goddess. When they examined the prisoners to be used as human sacrifice, they saw that the king's finger was missing. They let him go for they wanted a complete man as the human sacrifice. Then they examined the new prime minister. They found him fit for the sacrifice. Thus, the new prime minister was killed. The others were held back.

The king reached back to his palace. He asked the guards to free and fetch the imprisoned prime minister. The king said to him, "You were right. Whatever happens, happens for the good. I was saved due to my missing finger. You are free now. Now hold your post as usual."

The prime minister smiled, bowed low and said, "Yes, Your Majesty, whatever happens, happens for the good."

MORAL : Some problems or losses in our lives are for our own good.

The Hare and the Ass

A healthy, young ass was grazing on the green grass growing on a hill top. Unfortunately a hungry wolf saw him. He approached the ass and said, "Ah! You are such a juicy ass. I'll eat you for lunch."

The ass thought of saving his life, so he said, "Surely, sir, you can eat me but hear me out first. Come to meet me here, at the same spot one year from now. Then I'll be bigger, fatter and more juicy to eat."

The wolf was hungry but approved of the idea. So the wolf went away.

A year passed by. On the appointed day, the wolf was climbing up the hillside eager to go and eat the ass. A fox came by and asked, "Where are you rushing to, my friend?"

The wolf said, "A fat ass is waiting at the hilltop to be my lunch. Why don't you join me to enjoy the feast?"

The fox was hungry so she readily agreed to the idea. When the wolf and the fox were running to the hilltop, a hare came by. He asked, "Friends, where are you going ?" The fox replied, "We are going to enjoy ass meat for lunch. Would you like to join us ?"

The clever hare agreed and all the three soon reached where the ass was grazing. He had grown bigger and fatter. When the wolf was about to pounce on the ass, the clever hare said, "Please stop ! If you attack or cut him up, the ass will become a bloody mess. We won't be able to taste its juicy meat. I suggest we kill him by strangling his neck. I'll go and get a rope to tie and strangle his neck."

Soon the hare brought a rope. He made a large but loose noose at one end of the rope for the ass and two smaller nooses at the another end of the rope. The fox asked, "Why have you made the smaller nooses ?"

The hare said, "The large noose is for the ass. Each of the two small nooses I'll put round your neck. You must pull hard in opposite directions to tighten the noose round the neck of the ass. I'll hold the rope by my teeth so that the nooses round your neck don't tighten."

The fox, wolf and the ass had their nooses round their necks. Just as the fox and the wolf got their nooses, the hare let go of the rope. The ass ran down the hill. The pull caused the nooses to

tighten round the fox's and wolf's necks. The loose noose of the ass did not harm him. Thus, the two evil animals met their end.

MORAL : We must do our best to save others' lives.

The Jamun Tree

Ramu was a lazy young man. He did not do any work at all. One day as usual he was lazing under a tree near the field. He looked up at the tree and saw some juicy jamuns hanging from the branches. Then he looked into the field. He saw very large pumpkins growing on creepers. He started laughing very loudly and thought to himself, "Strange is the God's creation. This huge tree bears such tiny fruits and the large pumpkins grow on thin and tender vines. What a sight!"

A few minutes later as Ramu was still lying under the tree, a ripe jamun fell on him. The jamun hit Ramu's head. Ramu sat up and said, "Thank God, the pumpkins are not growing on this tree. If a pumpkin had fallen on my head instead of the jamun, I would have seen stars in daylight."

MORAL : Don't comment on things you know nothing about.

The Friendly Elephant

In a small village, Raja owned a tailor shop. He used to earn his living by sewing new and beautiful clothes for the villagers. Next to the tailor's shop, there was a temple on the road. It had an elephant. At every noon, the temple elephant used to go to the lake to take bath so he passed by Raja's shop daily. Raja loved elephants so he started offering bananas, sugar cane etc. to the elephant. Gradually, it became a habitual routine.

One day Raja had an argument with one of his customers. He was in a foul mood indeed. The temple elephant, of course, did not know anything about it. As usual, the elephant arrived at the shop and waited for Raja to offer him some eatables. Raja was angry and busy in work so he did not notice the elephant's arrival. After waiting for a few minutes, the elephant trumpeted loudly to get Raja's attention. This really irritated Raja so he took his needle and pricked it on the elephant's trunk. The elephant was in pain and confused at Raja's behaviour. But he went away as he was very hurt.

When the elephant was bathing in the lake he thought up an idea to teach Raja a lesson. As he left the lake, he filled his trunk with some dirty water. While passing by the Raja's shop, he splashed all the dirty water on the newly stitched dresses. Raja was also soaked from head to toe. He realized that the elephant had taken revenge for the way he had treated him. After that day many times Raja offered bananas to get the elephant's friendly nature back but he could not succeed. Thus, a beautiful friendship between Raja and the temple elephant came to an end.

MORAL : Never take out your anger on those who had done nothing to cause it.

Befriending the Jackal

A jackal and a deer lived in a forest. The jackal wanted to eat the deer but each time he tried to catch the deer, he would run away. As the jackal could not run as fast as the deer, he could not get his prey.

One day the jackal made up a plan. He went on the path the deer went past every day. He sat there and started crying loudly. The deer came by and saw the jackal crying. He enquired why the jackal was crying.

"I feel lonely as I have no friends. How can I live a friendless life ? I will go and drown myself in the river."

"You won't get a friend if you are dead. For that you must keep alive. From now onwards, I am your friend, so stop crying." the deer declared.

So the jackal and the deer became friends. A crow

who was the deer's friend asked him, "Who are you going around with?"

"That's my new friend, the jackal," the deer replied.

The crow said, "It's not right to become friends with anyone you know nothing about."

To this the jackal said, "Deer crow, even you did not know the deer very well when you befriended him. You only come to know each other well after you become close friends."

The crow did not say anything but he was worried about the deer.

One day the jackal took the deer to a large green field. The deer ate a lot of grass and roamed around. From that day both of them went together to the field everyday. The farmer, who owned the field, noticed that his crop was being damaged everyday. So the farmer laid out a net in which the deer got caught. The jackal felt happy. He thought

"Aha ! the deer is caught in a net. He would die soon and I would eat him up."

The crow had not seen the deer for some days. He flew around searching for his friend. He saw the deer in the field caught in a net. He flew down to the deer and said, "Don't worry, my friend ! Just lie down motionless as if you are dead. As soon as I call out, you must get up and run."

A while later, the farmer came to the spot. He saw the dead deer and set him free from the net. The crow called

out to the deer and the deer jumped up and ran off as fast as he could. The farmer threw a stick at the deer but it did not hit the deer. The jackal was hiding behind a bush. The stick struck the jackal's head and he died.

The deer realized that the crow was right. So the two friends lived happily ever after.

MORAL : Never trust a stranger.

Lazy Stomach

One day the various parts of the body started arguing. They all felt that the stomach was being given more importance than them.

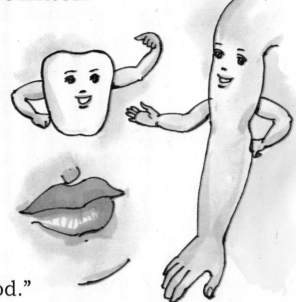

The teeth spoke up, "We chew the food for the stomach. He does not move an inch to get the food."

"No one appreciates the work we do," said the hands.

The legs asserted, "We walk all the time and what effort does the stomach make anyway ? He gets his food fixed where he is, yet everyone cares for him."

The tongue wagged, "Don't you see how people forever gives examples of the stomach in various sayings. No one cares how hard we work."

Thus each part of the body continued commenting about the stomach. So all of them decided to go on a strike. They stopped working.

The hand said, "I won't move even a finger."

"I won't take even a step," the leg claimed.

The teeth declared, "We'll stop chewing."

The mouth announced, "I'll not take a bite."

Poor stomach was listening and watching all that was going on. He was worried when he heard such silly comments. He felt pity for the parts of the body. He tried to talk to them but no one lent him a ear.

Now the stomach stopped getting food. As days went by, the body grew weak. Hands, legs, mouth, teeth and other parts did not receive any blood.

Then the stomach said, "What do I do ? Till I got the food, I used to send it to all of you. Now that I am not getting anything, how can I give strength to all of you?"

Now the parts of the body realized that, due to the stomach, they had been healthy and strong. They deserted him and were suffering now. They now knew that the stomach did work by taking food and giving them energy. He was not a useless fellow as they had thought.

So the body parts started working again. The hands and legs grew strong. The face shone with good health. The tongue started talking. So all of them got together to make a healthy body.

MORAL : Unity is strength.

Miser's Money

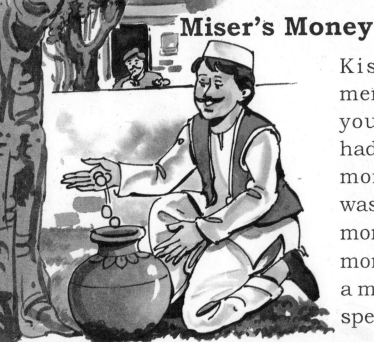

Kishan was a merchant. As a young man, he had earned a lot of money. Now he was old and had more than enough money but he was a miser. He did not spend his money.

As Kishan lived in a village, he felt it unsafe to leave his money in his house. So he spotted a peepal tree behind his house. He dug a hole under it and hid his pot full of money there. He was always scared that someone would steal his money. Every night he would dig out the pot from under the tree, count the money and hide it back.

One day Kishan's neighbour Ramu, grew suspicious. He thought, "Why does Kishan go to the back of his house each night ?"

So one night Ramu hid behind a wall and saw Kishan leave his house. Then he saw and understood what Kishan used to do every night.

Next day when Kishan had gone out, Ramu went to the peepal tree. He dug out the pot. He took out the money and placed pebbles in the pot. He took the money home.

That night, as usual, Kishan went to check his pot of money but he found pebbles in the pot. He started crying loudly. Hearing his cries many people and neighbours rushed to the spot. He kept crying, "Oh ! My money ! Someone has taken my money. What do I do now ?"

The village headman also arrived at the spot. He heard what had happened. So he said, "Kishan, it's no use crying now. The money you had kept in the pot were not being used by you. They were kept

there only to be counted. So, in fact, you have not lost anything. The thief has put pebbles in the pot for you to count. Counting money or counting pebbles, there is no difference as long as your counting does not stop."

Kishan realized that truly money, which was not being used was equal to pebbles, which are of no use.

MORAL : Being a miser invites miserable times.

Raghu Goes to Jail

Raghu was a very good student. He was a regular student and always did his daily home work. One day he thought, "My writing is beautiful. If I had a good pen, my writing will be even better."

He went home and said, "Mother, I want a good pen to write with."

His mother said, "Son, I can't give you a new pen now. We are poor and I don't have any money to buy a good pen for you."

The next day in school, one of Raghu's friend had gone out of the class. Raghu opened his bag and stole his new pen. He went home and showed it to his mother. His mother said, "Oh ! How clever you are, Raghu my son !" She did not scold or explain to him that stealing was wrong. So Raghu thought that as his stealing the pen had made his mother happy, so it was a right thing to do. Soon Raghu started stealing things from school and his neighbours' houses. But when each time someone complained to his mother, she would say, "My Raghu cannot be a thief at all. He is such a good and obedient son."

Years went by and Raghu grew into a young man but he had not let go of his bad habit. One night he entered a large mansion to steal some cash and ornaments. The owner of the mansion woke up and he and his servant caught Raghu red handed. Raghu was sent to the police station and a case was registered. Soon the case was heard in the criminal court. The judge reached the conclusion that Raghu must be put in prison.

Raghu's mother reached the prison. She was in tears. She went and hugged her son but, to her surprise, Raghu bit hard on her nose. She cried loudly. The guards took Raghu away from his mother. They asked him why he had bit on her nose. Raghu replied, "She is responsible for my imprisonment today. When I used to steal, people used to complain to her but at that time she used to protect me by taking my side. She never stopped me from stealing. She always took pride in what I stole and brought home. She has no right to feel sorry now."

MORAL : Children learn what their parents teach them.

The Donkey's Disguise

Once a washerman lived in a village. He had a donkey. The washerman was a miser, so he did not give enough food to the donkey. He used to make the poor animal work very hard. Soon the donkey grew weak and the washerman got worried about his health.

Once the washerman found a tiger skin lying on a forest path. He took it home with an idea in his mind. He covered the donkey with the tiger skin. Then at night, he let the donkey move in a field filled with standing crops.

That night when the farmer came to guard his field he got scared at the sight of a tiger in his field. Then he observed closely. He thought, "What is the tiger doing in my field ? Surely it hasn't come here to graze. He has been standing at the same spot for so long. Tigers never do this."

The farmer walked softly, went and hid behind a

tree near where the 'tiger' stood. He saw that it was a donkey in a tiger skin. To confirm further the farmer brayed loudly. Hearing this, the donkey in the tiger skin felt so happy that he also started braying. The farmer then took a stout stick and beat up the donkey till he was nearly unconscious.

Next morning when the washerman came to fetch the donkey, he felt very bad for the donkey. The farmer said to him, "A donkey remains a donkey even under a tiger skin."

The washerman felt that he had not treated his donkey well. From then onwards he took great care of his donkey.

MORAL : Showing off does not change what you truly are.

The Wet Monkey

One day it rained very heavily. All the animals and birds in Champak Vana sat safe and dry in their homes. Hares lived in their burrows, the snakes did not leave their holes, the squirrels kept peeping out of the tree holes.

A monkey was all wet with the rain water. He lived on trees so he did not have a house to live in. He was wet and was shivering in the cold. Cool winds were adding to his sorry state. Soon the monkey felt so cold that his teeth started chattering. Hearing this sound, a bird whose nest was on a leafy branch of the tree peeped out. She saw the monkey getting wet in the rain. She said, "Oh, dear monkey, you are so wet. If only you had built a home for yourself before the rains !"

The monkey said, "Will you keep shut ? I don't want your advise."

"But, dear friend, you have two hands like men so you could..."

"I told you I don't want to listen to you," the monkey grew angry.

"Oh dear, if only I had hands like yours...", the bird continued.

The monkey grew angrier, "If you say another word, I'll teach you a lesson."

But the foolish bird went on, "But I am telling you for your own good. If you had made a house before the rains, you would have not felt wet and cold now."

These words really made the monkey lose his temper. He was feeling irritated due to the rain and cold and the bird's constant patter was making him more and more irritated. The monkey climbed to the branch where the bird sat in her cosy nest. He took the bird's nest and throw it to the ground

and said, "You a tiny bird, you are as homeless and wet as I am. Do what you want to now."

The bird flew off to another leafy branch and thought, "It's no use giving advice to a fool."

MORAL : Advise those who would heed to it.

Praise be on the Lord

A very clever and intelligent king ruled a small kingdom. He was also a brave and just king. The whole country knew of his kind rule. But the king had a problem. He was fed up of his lying courtiers. They would never tire of falsely praising the king.

In the court everyday a courtier would claim, "Of all the kings who have ruled the land, you are the best."

The other one claimed, "There is no other king like you."

The third courtier declared, "There was never a king like you and will never be another."

The fourth courtier would announce, "You can command the wind to stop, stop the clouds from raining on earth and cause the tides in the oceans."

The king was tired of these false claims. One day he went on a stroll by the sea. The courtiers were with him. There were high waves in the sea. The tide was

in. The king said, "Courtiers, according to you am I truly the most powerful king in the world?"

"There's no doubt about it Your Majesty," all of them said in unison.

"Will you behave according to my orders?" asked the king to his courtiers.

"Why not? After all no one in this world is as powerful as you!"

"All right then," the king said. "Ask the guards to place my throne near the sea-shore. I will rest here a while."

Soon the throne was placed on the sea-shore. The courtiers stood around him.

The king said, "The tide is in. The waves are higher and coming nearer. If I order now will the sea stop from approaching towards me?"

The courtiers were scared. How could they say that it won't happen?

The king ordered. "O Sea, stop where you are. Don't let your waves near me."

But the tide came in. A small wave came and washed the king's feet. The king looked at the sea and said again. "O Sea, I am the strongest king of all. I order you to stop. If you don't, I'll teach you a lesson."

Just then a large, high wave came and drenched the king from head to toe. The king turned to the courtiers and said, "All of you claimed that no one in this world could disobey my orders as I am the most powerful of all kings. Then why didn't the sea stop? It's because the Lord is greater than me. No one is more powerful than Him, so if you want to rain praises, praise be on the Lord."

MORAL : Lord is all powerful.